To Malia
Follow Your Dreams.
Ahauta

MORE THAN A
Princess

BY SHAISTA PABLA
ILLUSTRATED BY DREW MAUNULA

Upon A Star Books
Toronto, ON

MORE THAN A PRINCESS

ISBN-13: 978-0-9951877-9-5

First print, September 2017

Printed in China

Edited by:
Allister Thompson

Published by:
Upon A Star Books
An imprint of Upon A Star Books Inc.
1859 Leslie St.
P.O. Box 36055
Toronto, ON
M3B 0A3
www.uponastarbooks.ca

To Maya and Aryan,
I promise to stand next to you for support,
in front of you to cheer you on,
and a few steps behind you to catch you if you fall.
I love you all the time, and some days...
– Mom

Once upon a time there was a princess named Maya. She was funny, brave, kind, and very smart. Princess Maya loved adventure more than anything and always wanted to learn new things and visit new places.

Now, just like any other princess, Princess Maya needed to marry a prince. Every day the king and queen would ask, "Maya, have you found your Prince Charming?" and every day Maya would respond, "I'm too busy looking for adventure to look for Prince Charming."

"But Maya, you're a princess, and you need to get married to a prince," her father would insist.

And every day Maya's answer would be the same: "Father, I'm more than a princess."

One day, a handsome prince named Oliver came to the castle and said, "Princess Maya, I would like to marry you."

He told her about his sparkly grey ship, his beautiful green countryside, and his enormous army of soldiers dressed in blue. "I have everything you need to be my queen," he told her. "Come with me, and you and I can rule my country together."

Well, Princess Maya was not impressed one bit. She shook her head.

"I don't need a sparkly grey ship, or a beautiful green countryside, or even an enormous army of soldiers dressed in blue. I want to travel the world and see things I have never seen and do things I have never done."

"I want to eat chocolate macarons in a café in Paris, France."

"I want to yell my name from the peak of Mount Kilimanjaro in Tanzania."

"I want to learn a language in a country I have only read about in books."

Princess Maya went on and on about the adventures she wanted to go on, and with each adventure her face got **brighter** and her smile got **bigger**.

But Prince Oliver was not impressed one bit.

He told the princess, "I don't want to do any of those things."

And Princess Maya replied calmly, **"Then I guess you're not the prince for me."**

So Prince Oliver left the castle in search of his princess, and Princess Maya continued her search for adventure.

A few days later, another handsome prince on a large white horse came to the castle to visit Princess Maya. His name was Prince Nicholas.

"Princess Maya, I would like to marry you," he told her, and then he went on about his beautiful enchanted palace and his elegant purple robes and his strong white horses.

"I have everything you need to be my queen," he said. "Come with me, and you and I can rule my country together."

Well, Princess Maya was not impressed one bit. She shook her head.

POP!

"I don't need a beautiful enchanted palace or elegant purple robes or even strong white horses. I want to travel the world and see things I have never seen and do things I have never done."

"I want to visit China and walk along the Great Wall."

"I want to hear my own echo at the Grand Canyon in Arizona."

"I want to learn how to hula dance in Hawaii."

Princess Maya went on and on about the adventures she wanted to seek, and with each adventure her face got **brighter** and her smile got **bigger**.

But Prince Nicholas was not impressed one bit.

He told the princess, "None of those things excite me."

And Princess Maya replied calmly, **"Then I guess you're not the prince for me."**

So Prince Nicholas left the castle in search of his princess, and Princess Maya continued her search for adventure.

This time weeks went by before another prince came to the castle to marry the beautiful princess. His name was Prince Aiden. He was very handsome and very rich, but he wasn't very nice. He told Princess Maya, "Princess, I would like you to marry me, and I will share everything I have with you."

He told her about his gold coins and his twinkling diamonds, and he promised her a shiny tiara with red rubies and glittering gems if she became his queen.

Well, Princess Maya was not impressed one bit.

She shook her head and said, "I don't need gold coins or twinkling diamonds or even a shiny tiara with red rubies and glittering gems. I want to travel the world and see things I have never seen and do things I have never done."

"I want to feel small standing next to the pyramids at Giza in Egypt."

"I want to learn how to scuba dive and swim with sharks in the Bahamas."

"I want to play with every colour of the rainbow during the Holi Festival in India."

Princess Maya went on and on about the adventures she wanted to seek, and with each adventure her face got **brighter** and her smile got **bigger**.

But Prince Aiden was not impressed one bit.

He told the princess, "All these adventures seem boring to me."

And Princess Maya replied calmly, **"Then I guess you're not the prince for me."**

Prince Aiden became very angry with Princess Maya, and because he wasn't a very nice prince, he made fun of her and laughed at her, calling her a **bad princess**.

This didn't bother Princess Maya at all. She knew in her heart that fairy tales and happily-ever-afters don't always have to include a handsome prince or a beautiful castle.

Even though some princesses dream of that, Princess Maya had other dreams for herself. She knew that this did not make her a bad princess, just a different princess with different dreams.

And knowing this made Princess Maya very happy as she continued her search for adventure.